a boy, a dog and a frog

by mercer mayer

dial books for young readers
new york

To my family,
Marianna and Samantha

Published by Dial Books for Young Readers
A division of Penguin Putnam Inc.
345 Hudson Street
New York, New York 10014

ISBN 978-0-8037-2880-6
Library of Congress Catalog Card Number: 67-22254
Manufactured in China on acid-free paper

14 15 16 17 18 19 20